The Alex Kilgour Joke Book

By Allan Cole

From The Sten Series
By Allan Cole And Chris Bunch

For Kathryn:
My one and only...
Without her persistence this book would not exist.

And To Chris
My late partner in crime.

The Alex Kilgour Jokebook
A Foreword:

The Sten series - read by millions across the planet - was nearly dead on arrival. To be completely accurate, it was very nearly dead before my late partner, Chris Bunch, and I were halfway through the first book.

This was to be our Novel debut - the realization of dreams that had begun for both of us when our ages were still in the single digits.

What the clot could be wrong?

We had a contract from Del Rey Books commissioned by none other than Judy Lynn del Rey herself. We had a thorough outline of the first book, plus outlines for eleven others. (As the years went by the 12 books we originally envisioned were pared to a leaner, meaner eight.) And at the point we sputtered to a halt we were two hundred damned pages into the book.

Each and every day, no matter how hard we tried, we just couldn't get our Sten mojo going. We'd sit hunched over our keyboards, brows furrowed so deep you could have planted whole fields of turnips. Then one of us would groan, the other would moan, and we'd quit and break out the Scotch.

One day Chris made a depressing admission. "The trouble is," he said, "is that I've started to hate the little bugsnipe."

I didn't have to think long before I came to the same realization. I just didn't give a horse's fat patootie about Sten one way or the other. And I was one of his creators, for clot's sake!

4

Allan Cole

Chris said, "Here we have this kid whose parents we kill at the very beginning of the story."

"And his brother and sister," I said. "Don't forget them.'

Chris snorted. "How could I frigging ever? He won't let me." Then he said, "We've got two hundred pages of this little buttwipe dragging around, going Boo-Hoo, Woe Is Frigging Me. I'm so sad and lonely I could kill myself."

" I wouldn't care if he did," I added, my depression deepening. I was beginning to see the light at the end of the tunnel and it was an oncoming train.

"He's like effing Oliver Twist," Chris said. "Moping around all the time so it gets so you want to kick his butt yourself. Dump the bowl of porridge over his head and stomp on his toes when he asks, 'Please, Sir, just a littl more.'"

"Yeah, it's the Artful Dodger you root for, not little Ollie." I said. "The Dodger's had an even worse life, but he's always out there on the street laughing and hollering and cutting every purse in sight. He's a nasty piece of work. But much more likable than Dicken's darling orphan."

A long silence followed. We replenished our Scotches - more J&B than Schweppes, because you really have to watch your sodium intake, don't you know?

Finally, Chris sat up - light dawning. And intoned: "He was born with the gift of laughter and a sense that the world was mad."

I nodded, remembering. "Rafael Sabatini," I said. "Scaramouche. One of the best first sentences ever. Not quite up there with 'Call me Ishmael,' or 'Turkey Doolin's crotch itched but close."

"That's our problem," Chris said. "Sten is a humorless little son of a bitch. That's what we have to fix."

We thought on it long and hard, then made a very tough decision. One of the hardest ever for a writer.

We dumped two hundred damned pages into the trash. (All except for the opening sentence, which is pretty good as first sentences go: "Death came quietly to The Row.)

And started all over again.

Except this time we gave Sten - and the series - a sense of humor. It's dark humor, to be sure. The humor of cops, soldiers, coroners, and desperate writers.

After the first book, Alex Kilgour- Sten's heavyworlder sidekick - assumed the major burden with his incredibly awful jokes told in an impenetrable Scottish accent. But before we could get to Alex, we had to change the whole tone of the series.

The first moment - and turning point - comes in Sten #1, when our hero is condemned to the Exotics Section - an area known by the denizens who work and died there, as Hellworld.

The book that follows is the brainchild of Kathryn, my wife, and my late partner's sister. She's gathered together all the jokes - with the scenes surrounding them - that we could find. Unfortunately, there are a couple missing - the eight novels run over a million words so it's harder to find something than you might think, even with the aid of computers.

Allan Cole

The Alex Kilgour Joke Book

I've reconstructed those jokes from old Sten notes, plus added others that Chris and I wrote, but had to scrap for reasons of space. I'm calling it The Alex Kilgour Toxic Scrapheap for obvious reasons.

Stregg Forever, Allan Cole (Boca Raton, Fl. 2011)

STEN #1

The Book:

Vulcan is a factory planet, centuries old, Company run, ugly as sin, and unfeeling as death. Vulcan breeds just two types of native — complacent or tough. Sten is tough. When his family is killed in a mysterious accident, Sten rebels, harassing the Company from the metal world's endless maze-like warrens. He could end up just another burnt–out Delinq. But people like Sten never give up.

*****

The Setup:

Our hero is befriended by a Hite, a fellow Hellworld inmate with a mysterious background that includes an education both in medicine and street fighting on the deadliest level. It is Hite who teaches Sten how to survive. How to fight. How to use cunning and guile. He helps Sten create a marvelous knife that is surgically implanted in a fleshy sheath. But, most of all, Hite teaches Sten how to laugh.

The Scene:

"Sten, lad. The problem with you is you don't laugh enough."

"Laugh? I'm stuck in the anus of Vulcan...everybody's trying to kill me - they're gonna succeed - and you want me to laugh?"

"Of course, boy. Because what could be funnier than all that?"

"I don't get it."

Hite leaned closer. "It's because the gods hate you. Personally."

Sten considered. Then smiled slowly. And started laughing.

"There's your other problem, boy. You laugh too much."

"Huh?"

"What's there to laugh about? You're up the arse of Vulcan and everyone's trying to kill you. I'd get worried if I were you."

Sten stared at him. Then shook his head and started howling.

Allan Cole

From The Alex Kilgour Toxic Scrapheap

The Setup:

This joke was originally intended for the segment where Sten is being trained as an Imperial Guardsman. But that section was running perilously long, so we cut it. The story was to be told by one of Sten's mates over a few narco-beers.

The Joke:

A green troopie was on sentry duty at the main gate. The orders from his sergeant were clear. "Maggot!" barked Lanzata. "Mark this, and mark it clottin' well. No Gravcar may enter the camp without an official holo pass on the windguard."

"Yes, Sergeant!" bellowed the recruit, scared spitless by the snarling behemoth of a woman.

"And there will be no exceptions, 'Cruit," growled Lanzata. "Screw this up, and I'll have your scrote for breakfast. And a very small breakfast it will be. Do you understand me, maggot!"

"Yes, Sergeant," cried the troopie.

"If anyone, tries to pass without authorization you are to shoot, maggot! And I mean shoot, to kill! Do you clottin' understand me, 'Cruit!"

Shaking in his boots, the troopie bawled, "The maggot understands, sergeant. Shoot to kill. No exceptions."

Sgt. Lanzata hadn't been gone more than a millisecond, when up purrs a big, black staff gravcar. In the back, was General Clottinheimer, himself. Up front is the chauffeur, a lowly corporal.

10

Allan Cole

Our green troopie stiffens to attention, rifle held smartly. Then, recalling his duty, he examins the gravcar. And lo and behold there's not a holo pass in sight.

The gravcar inches forward and the troopie bars the way. "Halt," he shouts. "Who goes there?"

The corporal at the gravcar's controls shouts back: "General Clottinheimer!"

Hearing that name and that exalted rank, the young soldier is so scared he's ready to drakh his britches, but he even more scared of Sgt. Lanzata.

Voice quivering, he says, "I'm sorry. I can't let you enter. You don't have a holo pass on your windguard."

Gen. Clottinhemier's face turns red with fury. He bellows at his corporal, "Drive on!"

But the young sentry is adamant. "Halt!" he shouts as the gravcar edges forward. Then, more reasonably, "You really can't come through here. I have orders to shoot if you try driving on without a holo pass. No exceptions."

The general isn't having any of this. He pokes the corporal with his swagger stick. "I'm ordering you, Corporal - drive on!"

The sentry doesn't know what to do. Finally, he walks to the rear window to confront the commander.

"General, sir," he said, brave as could be. "I'm new at this. Do I shoot you or the driver?"

Allan Cole

Enter The Scotsman:

The character of Alex Kilgour was introduced in the first Sten, but it wasn't until the Wolf Worlds that he really came into his own and we unleashed his special brand of humor - shaggy dog stories that would sometimes be spread across not just one book, but two.

After Wolf Worlds, Chris and I made the Kilgour shaggy dog stories an integral part of the Sten formula. We made it a rule that we had to have at least one Kilgour type joke in every book. We spent the months in between each Sten collecting suitable jokes, then when the time came we'd pick the best - which in Kilgour's case meant it had to be the worst.

Sometimes we couldn't decide and in the first rough draft of the book we'd put in a whole passel of jokes. Then, when the final draft was written, we'd make the hard choice of which would stay, and which would be banished to The Alex Kilgour Toxic Scrapheap.

As a disservice to you, Gentle Reader, I am including the worst of those trashed jokes.

A side note: The character of Alex Kilgour was based on a real life Scotsman, who also went by that name. The real Alex Kilgour was a retired SAS soldier. (Strategic Air Services - The UK's elite commandos, arguably the best fighters in the world). Like the fictional Kilgour, he was short, tubby, immensely strong and amazingly fast. Chris befriended him while vacationing in Scotland and I became acquainted with Alex when he visited Chris in the U.S. (For the full skinny see My Hollywood

Allan Cole

The Alex Kilgour Joke Book

MisAdventures - Episode #42, Alex Kilgour In Hollywood http://allan-cole.blogspot.com/2010/07/alex-kilgour-in-hollywood.html)

One other thing: The Real Alex Kilgour was also addicted to shaggy dog stories, many of which appeared in the Sten series.

And now on to:

Allan Cole

STEN #2 - The Wolf Worlds

The Book:

Raised on the factory planet of Vulcan, Sten soon learns about the survival of the toughest. Now he wants more than survival. The Eternal Emperor rules countless worlds across the galaxy. Vast armies and huge fleets await his command. But when the Emperor needs to pacify the Wolf Worlds, the planets of the insignificant Lupus Cluster that have raised space piracy to a low art, he turns to his Mantis Team and its small band of militant problem–solvers. Sten's destiny is in his own hands.

The Setup:

This joke was told by The Real Alex Kilgour. In the story Sten and his Mantis Team are dispatched by the Eternal Emperor to settle a religious dispute that is likely to end in all out warfare. The trouble is there are three Pope-like beings who are at each other's throats. The Emp doesn't much care who comes out on top, as long as the conflict doesn't interrupt Imperial trade. It is in the Wolf Worlds that we also introduce the Bhor - an incredibly violent breed of warriors whose favorite drink is Stregg - a booze so strong that the drinker's breath would stop a charging Banth in its tracks.

The Joke:

(Scene One - Alex killing time as their spacecraft hurtles toward certain doom)

Alex broke in. The tubby three-gee-world Scotsman was sprawled on his accel couch. He'd insisted that if he were going to die, he was going to die in uniform. And the others agreed.

"It wae back ae Earth... ane, b'fore the Emp'ror, even. In those days, m'ancestors wae called Highlanders, aye."

"Twelve minutes, even, and closing," Ida announced flatly.

"Now, in th' elder days, tha' Brits wae enemies. E'en tha, we Scots ran th' Empire tha had, wi'out tha' known it."

In spite of the tension, Sten got interested.

"Howinhell, Alex, can anybody run an empire without the boss knowing about it?"

"Ten minutes to atmosphere," Doc said.

"Ah 'splain thae some other time, lad. So, one braw day, there's this reg'mint ae Brit guards, aw braw an' proud in their red uniforms an' muskits. An' th' walkin' along thro' this wee glen, wi' they band playin' an' drumits crashin' an singin' and carryin' on, an' all ae sudden, they hears this shout frae th'crags abouve 'em. 'Ah'm Red Rory a' th' Glen!'

"An' th' Brit general 'e looks up th' crag, an' here's this braw enormous Highlander, wi' his kilt blowin' an' his bearskin o'er one shoulder an' aye this braw great claymore in his hand. 'E has this great flowit beard on him.

Allan Cole

"An' yon giant, 'e shouts just again, 'Ah'm Red Rory a' th' Glen! Send oop y'best pickit man.'

"An' so the Brit gen'rl turns to his adj'tant an' says,' Adj'tant! Send up our best man. Ah wan' tha' mon's head!'"

"Hold on the story," Ida cut in coldly. "We're on launch." Dead silence in the control room… except for the increased panting of the lashed-down tigers.

(Much Later -The joke continues with Otho, the Bhor Chieftain)

Otho watched the screen time-tick seconds until dropaway with half his attention. The other half was listening to the droned story from behind him, coming from the humanoid that Otho sometimes found himself wishing to be a Bhor:

"Ahe," Alex went on. "'S' th' Brit gin'ral hae order't ae squad up tha' hill f 'r Red Rory's head. An' aye, a pickit squad wan' roarin' upit tha' hill.

"An tha's screekit an' scrawkit' an' than, bumpit, bumpit, bumpit, doon tha' hill comit th' heads ae th' squad.

"An' th' Brit gin'ral lookit up tha' hill, an' on th' crest still standit thae giant.

"An' he skreekit, 'Ah'm Red Rory ae th' Glen! Send up y'r best comp'ny!'

"An" th' Brit gin'ral turnit a wee shade more purple, an' he say, 'Adj'tant!' An' th' adj'tant sae, 'Sah!'

"An' th' Brit gin'ral sae, 'Adj'tant, send up y'r best comp'ny! Ah wan' tha' man's head!

"The adj'tant sae' Sah!'

16

Allan Cole

"An' he sendit oop th' hill th' reg'mint's best comp'ny!"

And the timeclick went to zero and Otho touched the button. Alex cut his story off as the Bhor captain got busy...

*****

(Still Later: The Mantis Team prepares for the final assault on Sanctus, the heavily guarded fortress of their enemy. As they await certain death, Alex takes the opportunity to return to Red Rory...)

"Sharrup, lass," Alex replied. "Ah'm dooncast. Ah fearit this scheme wi' nae workit oot f r th' benefits of Kilgours."

"You're probably right," Sten agreed. "We're doomed. And doomed without hearing the last of Red Rory."

"Red Rory, aye?" And Alex brightened. "W'noo. Wh'n last w'sawit Red Rory, an entire Brit comp'ny wae chargint up thae hill, a'ter his head, aye?"

Sten nodded wearily. The things he did to keep morale up.

"So tha' screekit, an' scrawit, an' hollerint, and ae kinds ae goin' on, an' then heads come doon thae hill, bumpit, bump-it, bumpit.

"Anh t' thae Brit gin'ral's consid'r'ble astonishment, here's his wholit comp'ny, lyin' dead in thae dust.

"But b'fore he hae a chance to consider, yon giant on tha hillcrest screekit again:

"'Ah'm Red Rory ae th' Glen! Send up y' entire rig'mint!'"

An the gin'ral turnit sa red hi' adj'tant fearit he gae apoplexy. An' he holler, 'Adj'tant!'

Allan Cole

"'Send up tha' wholit blawdy reg'mint! AH WAN' THA' MON'S HEAD!'

"An' tha' whole reg'mint fixit thae bay'nits an' thae chargit up thae hill. An' thae's screamint, an' screekit, an' shoutint, an' carryint on, for aye half ae day.

"An' thae's dust, an' thae's shots, an' thae's aye battle. "An' th' gin'ral's watchint frae doon below.

"Ah sudden, thro' thae dust, he see't his adj'tant comit runnin doon thae hill.

"An' tae adj'tant screemit. 'Run, sah! Run! It's ae ambush!

"Thae's two ae 'em.'"

Very complete silence for many minutes.

Finally Sten turned to Alex, incredulous. "You mean, that's the story I've been waiting for, for the last year?"

"Aye," Alex said. "Dinnae it b'wonderful?"

Even more and longer silence…

*****

The Alex KilgourToxic Scrapheap

Strictly speaking, this isn't from one of the books. I liked the joke when I heard it, and wrote it up as a tale from the Eternal Emperor for the enjoyment of a few online friends. I envision the joke taking place near the beginning of The Wolf Worlds, after the Emp has returned from a fishing vacation. One

18

Allan Cole

cheat: I introduced Stregg before it was mentioned in the books. And who among you wouldn't?

The Eternal Emperor's Fish Story:

"How was the fishing, boss?" asked Ian Mahoney, the Eternal Emperor's right hand man. He knew the answer, of course. But out of politeness he had to ask. As head of security he knew everything the Emperor did, and that included his fishing trip to his estate on old Earth, which included what had once been the state of Oregon.

"It was a good holiday, but a strange one," the Emperor said, topping off his mug of Stregg and pushing the bottle over to Ian.

"Strange how, boss?" Ian asked, filling up his own mug and taking a tentative drink. The fiery Bhor liquid hit bottom and bounced a couple of times, then settled in so its warmth could spread.

"Well, you know I love to fish for bass, so I spent a small fortune stocking my lake with those bad boys," the Emperor said. "They can give you a helluva fight. I was eager to get out and at them, but that Lupus Cluster business descended on me so I was busy for a few cycles."

He lowered the level of his mug, wiped his mouth, and filled it up again to the brim. Offered it to Mahoney, who shook his head. Not yet. His belly was still roiling.

"Anyway, I finally got out to the lake and settled in," the Emperor continued. "The fish were jumping like a twenty-foot Gurion was after them, but they kept shaking loose of my line.

19

"Finally, I ran out of bait. I looked around to see what I could do, and saw a cottonmouth swimming by with a fat frog in his mouth. I'm thinking, with a frog in his mouth he can't bite me. So I grab him behind the head, get the frog loose and dump it in my bait bucket.

"Then I realize that I'm in real trouble. How do I let go of the snake without it biting me? Then I see my flask of Stregg, get it out, get the cap off with my teeth and I pour a few drops into the snake's mouth.

"Well, his eyes rolled up and he looks kind of dazed so I put him in the water and he swims away. No harm done and I get back to fishing."

"That was quick thinking, boss," Mahoney marveled.

"But you haven't heard the whole thing," the Emperor said. "I was sitting there fishing away, when all of a sudden I feel a bump against my boot. I look down, and lo and behold it's that clottin' snake!

"Except this time he has two frogs in his mouth."

A long time later, when Mahoney finished laughing, he wiped his eyes, then had a thought.

"Wait a minute, boss," he said. "Since when did they have cottonmouth snakes in Oregon?"

The Emperor fixed him with a royal stare. "Are you casting doubt on my fish story, Ian?"

"No sir. Not me. Never crossed my mind. Here, boss... how about another round of Stregg?"

Allan Cole

And so they finished that bottle, cracked another, and toasted old friends and fish stories.

*****

From The Alex Kilgour Toxic Scrapheap

The Setup:

While trying to settle on which "Pope" will end up running The Lupus Cluster, Sten and Alex put together a mercenary army funded by one of their "clients." The recruits are not only from different worlds - and species - but from different branches of the military. All traditional enemies, even when allied. Alex and Sten are hard put to get everyone straightened out and reading from the same fiche.

The Joke:

Alex has just stopped into a brawl over which was the superior service , knocked heads together, then sat the combatants down, poured Narcobeer all around, then told this tale for their edification:

"A marine general, an army general an' a navy admiral waur discussin' fa hud th' tooghest men. Th' army general says, 'Alrecht, I'll prove th' army has th' tooghest men in all th' Empire. He shouts: "Private, gie ower haur!"

The private reports as ordered, "Yes sairrr?"

The general says, "See 'at soldier ower thaur? Kill heem!"

Withit hesitatin', th' private kills th' poor mon.

The general says to th' oth'rs, "See? 'At cheil has balls!"

Allan Cole

The marine general says, "That's naethin'. Private, gie ower haur!"

The marine private reports, "Yes, sairrr?"

The marine general says, "See 'at cheil ower thaur? Kill heem an' then kill yerself."

Withit blinkin', th' marine private pulls ought his willy-gun an' blows away th' guy, 'en turns th' rifle oan himself an' unloads a roond into his head.

"The marine general says, "See? Noo 'at cheil has real balls!"

The admiral says, "That's naethin'."

He calls tae a seaman high up oan a tower, "Yey, seaman! Jump aff that tower!"

The seaman answers, "Excuse me, sairrr?"

The admiral repeats, "Jump aff 'at tower!"

The seaman replies, "Clot ye, sairrr!"

The admiral says, "See? 'At cheil has balls an' he's got brains too!"

*****

When Chris and I were working in Hollywood we made frequent use of the Army Film Liaison offices. There were always at least six jokers staffing the office staff at any one time. One day we saw a poster on the wall. Title: Murphy's Laws Of Combat Operations. Immediately we vowed to steal them and adapt them for Sten.

Along about the Wolf Worlds we thought we had a good place for them and at one point they were even in the book -

22

Allan Cole

posted on a barracks room wall. But, by the time The Wolf Worlds hit the presses they were gone -cut for space.

So, here they are now in all their bleak - but hilarious - glory.

STEN'S LAWS OF COMBAT OPERATIONS

Friendly fire - isn't.

Recoilless rifles - aren't.

Suppressive fires - won't.

A sucking chest wound is Nature's way of telling you to slow down.

If it's stupid but it works, it isn't stupid.

Try to look unimportant; the enemy may be low on ammo and not want to waste a bullet on you.

Never forget that your weapon was made by the lowest bidder.

If your attack is going really well, it's an ambush.

The enemy invariably attacks on two occasions: when they're ready and when you're not.

Five second fuses always burn three seconds.

The easy way is always mined.

Teamwork is essential; it gives the enemy other people to shoot at.

Never draw fire; it irritates everyone around you.

If you are short of everything but the enemy, you are in the combat zone.

When you have secured the area, make sure the enemy knows it too.

Allan Cole

Sten #2 - The Wolf Words

Incoming fire has the right of way.

No combat ready unit has ever passed inspection.

If the enemy is within range, so are you.

The only thing more accurate than incoming enemy fire is incoming friendly fire.

Things which must be shipped together as a set, aren't.

Com units will fail as soon as you need fire support.

Anything you do can get you killed, including nothing.

Make it too tough for the enemy to get in, and you won't be able to get out.

Tracers work both ways.

Professional soldiers are predictable; the world is full of dangerous amateurs.

Fortify your front; you'll get your rear shot up.

Weather ain't neutral.

If you can't remember, the Claymore is pointed towards you.

Mines are equal opportunity weapons.

The one item you need is always in short supply.

Interchangeable parts aren't.

It's not the one with your name on it; it's the one addressed "to whom it may concern" you've got to think about.

When in doubt, empty your magazine.

The side with the simplest uniforms wins.

If you can keep your head while those around you are losing theirs, you may have misjudged the situation.

Whenever you lose contact with the enemy, look behind you.

Allan Cole

The Alex Kilgour Joke Book

The most dangerous thing in the combat zone is an officer with a map.

The quartermaster has only two sizes, too large and too small.

If you really need an officer in a hurry, take a nap.

There is nothing more satisfying than having someone take a shot at you, and miss.

Close only counts in horseshoes and hand grenades.

The enemy always times his attack to the second you squat on the Loo.

Allan Cole

STEN 3 - Court Of A Thousand Suns

The Book:

Sten had fought his way up from slave labor on a factory world to commander of the Eternal Emperor's bodyguard, the Imperial Gurkhas. But during his first three months on Prime World, the most dangerous weapons Sten had encountered were the well–phrased lies of Court politicians. It seemed no place for an honest fighting man. But when a bomb destroys a local bar, Sten discovers the danger and corruption behind Court intrigue. Only quick work by Sten, Alex Kilgour, and a tough female detective can keep the Empire together and the Emperor alive.

*****

The Setup:

This twisted tale is another original from the Real Alex Kilgour. In this scene, Sten and Alex - who are hot on the trail of the man responsible for killing the Emperor's favorite Joygirl - are posing as guards on a Dru - a prison planet named after my younger, red-headed brother, Drew. Reluctantly, Sten agrees to Alex's plan to distract the other guards with one of his horrible stories, while Sten does some sneaky stuff.

The Joke:

Step One was Alex's story. "Ah," he mock-yawned. "Nae a month on Dru, an a'ready Ah heard y'r best stories."

"You got a better one, Ohlsn," a guard jeered. The tubby Scotsman had already established himself as a character and a favorite among the guards. Especially since he was more than willing to buy his round and another.

"Since Ah'm buyin't, shouldna ye be shuttin' y'r mouth?"

Silence fell.

"Ah'm tellin't a story aboot Old Earth. Before e'en the Emperor. Back when we Scots ran free an' bare-leggit on a wee green island.

"But e'en then, afore the Emperor, there was an Empire. Romans, they were call't. An because they were sore afrait a' the wee Scots, they built this braw great wall across the island. Wi' us on one side, an' them on the other.

"Hadrian's Wall, it was namit.

"But e'en then, bus'ness was bus'ness. So a' course, tha' were gates in th' wall, for folks to go backit an' forth.

"A' course there were guards on th' gate.

"On th' evenin' in question, there wa' two guards on th' wall, Marcus and Flavius... "

*****

(There's an interruption as Sten and Alex are nearly discovered. Then things relax again, and Sten resumes his sneaky work while Alex resumes his story...)

*****

Allan Cole

"... Now here's Marcus, who's been on this wee isle for years an' years. But puir Flavius, he's only been there for a month or so. An' the puir lad's scarit solid. He dinna like th' food, he dinna like th' weather, an' most a' all, he's messin' his tunic aboot th' Scots.

"'Dinna Fash,' Marcus tells him. 'Aboot nine a' th' evenin't, y'll be hearin't a braw whoopin't an' hollerin't an' carryin't on.

"'Tha'll just be the Scots comin't oot a' th' grogshops. But y'll noo have to worry.'

"But Flavius is worryin'... "

Sten was also worrying. He looked around - every eye in the rec room seemed intent on Alex's story.

Sten slithered a microdrill from his pocket and touched it to the rear of the game machine. The drill whined in. Sten plugged the connection on the drill handle into an outlet on the microbluebox and keyed the analysis button. The blue-box hummed concernedly.

"... So noo it's nigh nine, and sure enow, there's whoopin't an hollerin't an' carryin't on. And aye, doon the street toward our wee Romans comit this braw great cluster a' Scots. An' they're hairy an' dirty an' wearin't bearskins and carryin't great axes a' claymores.

"And Flavius knows he's gone to die here on this barren isle light-years from his own't beautiful Rome. So he's shakin't an' shiverin't.

"But Marcus, he's got this braw smile on his face a' this horrible horde comit staggerin't up.

Allan Cole

"'Evenin', he says.

"'Clottin' Romans,' comit th' growl, an' somebody unlimbers a sword.

"'You're lookin't good a' this night,' Marcus goes on.

"'Clottin' Romans' is th' solo thing he gets back, an' th' Scots are e'en closer, an' Flavius can smell their stinki't breath, an' he's a dead mon.

"'Nice night tonight,' Marcus keeps goin't.

"'Clottin' Romans,' comes again.

"Flavius hae his wee eyes shut, not wantin't' see the blade tha' rips his guts out an' all. But nae happen't.

All th' braw hairy killer monskers pass through the gate.

"An Flavius is still alive.

"He relaxes then. Takit twa deep breaths, grins a' Marcus, an' says, 'Y're right. Tha Scots na be so bad.'

"'Aye, lad. You're learnin,' Marcus comes back. 'But in another hour, when their men get done drinkin't, p'raps there'll be a wee spot a' trouble." '

As usual when Alex finished one of his stories, there was uncomprehending silence.

*****

The Setup:

After getting the things they need to go undercover, there is some very necessary work to be done. Like making false ID's - with phony records to back them - and the creation of the disguises themselves. This task falls to Sten. And what happens to him comes from something that actually happened to Chris

29

Allan Cole

when he was using glue and Velcro to attach the sheath of his boot knife to the boot.

The Joke:

"Alex, help," Sten said plaintively.

"A min, lad. A min. Ah'm lockit up noo." Alex was indeed quite busy in the tiny slum flat they'd rented. Kilgour was feeding the ID cards, personal photos, and such from Keet and Ohlsn into one of the few Mantis tools they'd brought with them. The machine was copying the ID cards and personal data from the two originals then altering them so that Sten and Alex's pictures and physical characteristics were implanted on the documents.

"Sergeant Major Kilgour, I still outrank you, damn it!"

The final photo clicked out a shot of Keet, arm in arm with some female-by-courtesy who must have been the love of his life. The new photo, however, showed Sten as the erring lover. Kilgour beamed and fingered a button. The machine began hissing — in less than a half a minute the original documents in the machine, and the guts of the machine itself, would be a nonanalyzable chunk of plas. He turned to see what Sten's problem was.

"I am not," he said firmly, "a clottin' seamstress. I am a captain in the Imperial Guard. I do not know how to sew. I do not know how to alter uniforms to fit, even with sewing glue and this clottin' knife. All I know how to do is glue my fingers together."

30

Allan Cole

Kilgour tsked, poured himself a now off-duty drink, and sadly surveyed Sten.

"How in hell did y'manage to glue both hands together? M'mum w'd nae have trouble wi' a simple task like that."

Before Sten could find a way to hit him, Alex solved the problem by dumping his mug of alk over Sten's hands, dissolving the sewing glue, which Sten had rather ineptly been using to retailor Keet and Ohlsn's uniforms. The mug was swiftly refilled and handed to Sten, who knocked it back in one shot.

"Ah," Alex pointed out wisely after Sten had finished choking and wiping the tears from his eyes. "Y've provit th' adage."

Sten just stared lethally at his partner.

"Ah y'sew, tha's how y'weep."

Kilgour, Sten decided, was definitely rising above his station.

*****

The Setup:

Two jokes from the Real Alex Kilgour made it into "Court." We come in on Sten and Alex, who are on yet another deadly mission - this time to get aboard a heavily guarded warship to save the Emperor and his Tahn diplomat guests from assassination. As the tension mounts, Alex falls back on humor to ease things up for his Gurkah comrades.

Allan Cole

The Joke:

"I did not know, Sergeant Major, you were aware of just who your ancestors were," Naik Gunju Lama said in seeming innocence.

Kilgour sneered at him. "Frae off'cers Ah hae't'take drakh like tha', but no frae a wee private who hae to gie back to Katmandu to have his pubes pulled.

"As ae was sayin't, Captain. One ae m'ancestors went on th' dole, an'— "

"What the hell's a dole?" Sten asked. There'd been no signals from his remotes, and so they had time to kill. Listening to another of Kilgour's absurd stories seemed as good a way to pass the time as any.

"A wee fruit, shaped like a pineapple. Now dinna be interruptin' me, lad. So it's necessary tha' m' ancestor sees a quack, to certify he's nae able to ply his trade.

"The doc looks a' m' ancestor, one Alex Selkirk Kilgour, an' blanches. 'Lad,' he says. 'Y' be missin't parts!'

"M' ancestor says, 'Aye.'

"'Why'd y' nae hae transplants?'

"'It was nae possible,' Selkirk explains. 'Y' see, till recent, Ah was a pirate.'

"The doc thinkit tha' makit sense, an proceeds wi' th' exam. Whae he's done, he says, 'Sir, y'be't healthy aye a MacDonald.'

"'Exceptin' tha' missin't parts.'

Allan Cole

"So Selkirk, he explain'it: 'Y'see't tha' missin't leg? Wi' the peg? Ah was boardin't a richun's yacht, an' th' lock door caught me.'

"Th' medico listen't, mos' fascinated.

"'The hook?' Selkirk gie on, 'Tha' be from't ae laser blast. Took m' paw off clean't ae whistle.'

"'An' the eye?' the doc asks.

"Selkirk, e' fingers th' patch. Th' eye? Tha's frae seagull crap.'

"Th' wee surgeon's a' puzzled an' all.

"'Seagull crap?'

"'Aye. Ah was in th' dockyard, starin't up ae a crane, an a gull go't o'er an' deposits in me eye.'

"'But how can seagull crap.... '

"'Ah, doctor, y'see, Ah'd only had the hook twa days.' "

Sten fought for the proper response and then found it. "Clottin' Romans!" And then he focused his attention back on the warning screens.

*****

The Setup:

Hot on the trail of a suspect, Sten and Alex track a rogue medic to the mining planet of Kulak, populated by very tough miners. The sheriff was even tougher - Jill Sherman, "the only law on Kulak." (Trivia: She was named for one of our producer friends on The Incredible Hulk TV series, starring Bill Bixby and Lou Ferrigno.) Naturally, in the course of things the miners all

Allan Cole

go after Sten and Alex. Our heavyworlder must head them off while Sten goes after the bad guy. And in the middle of the brawl, Alex has a hankering to recite Horatio At The Gate - in his fashion.

The Joke:

And there was nothing that Kilgour enjoyed more than a vulgar brawl. In motion, he looked like a heavily armored ball that ricocheted away from the lock entrance to connect with a target and then spun back to position, an armored ball confusedly quoting half-remembered and terrible poetry.

"Tha' oot spake braw Horatius.

Th' cap' ae th' gate:

T' every man upon the airt,

A fat lip cometh soon or late."

The fat lip was a miner's smashed faceplate and a near-fatal concussion.

Alex was too busy to see the man fall as he grabbed a swinging, grab-iron-wielding arm and shoved the grab iron into a third miner's gut, exploding the pressurized suit.

"Ae Astur's throat Horatius

Right fi rmly pressed his heel . . ."

That miner gurgled into oblivion.

"An' thrice an four times tugged amain . . ."

..."Sorry lad for the poetic license..."

"Ere he wrenched out the steel."

Allan Cole

The miners pulled back to regroup. Alex turned his suit oxy supply to full and waited. The mob — only half of it was still interested in fi ghting — grew hesitant.

"Wae none who would be foremost

To lead such dire attack;

But those behind criet 'forrard.'

An' thae before cried for their wee mums."

That was too much, and the miners phalanxed forward. A phalanx works very well, so long as nobody takes out the front rank. Alex went fl at in the dome's muck and rolled toward the onrushing miners. The front rank stumbled and went down, effectively blocking the airlock.

And Alex was running amok in their rear. The ram of his helmet was as effective as his feet and fists, and then the mob was hesitating, turning, and running down the narrow passageways, away from Alex.

He collected himself, chopped his suit's air supply, and opened hisfaceplate, breathing deeply to let the euphoria and adrenaline ebb somewhat.

"It stands some'eres or other

Plain for all to see.

Wee Alex in his kilt an' socks

Dronk upon one knee

An' underneath is written

In letters ae of mold

How valiantly he kept th' bridge

Ee the braw days ae old."

Allan Cole

Alex looked around, hoping for an appreciative audience. There was none — the battle casualties were either terminal, moaning for a medico, or crawling away at speed. But Alex wasn't bothered.

"Tha," he went on, "wa a poem Ah learn't a' m' mither's knee an' other low joints."

*****

The Setup:

Holed up in their safehouse - The Blue Bhor - Sten is sicker than a reek-sprayed cur. Alex, of course, is anxious to appear sympathetic.

The Joke:

"Are y' finished, wee Sten," Alex inquired gently.

Sten coughed and straightened from the commode. Too quickly; his guts spasmed and he heaved again.

"Advice, lad," Kilgour went on. "When y' feel a wee furry ring comin't up on y', swallow fast, since it's y'r bung."

*****

The Setup:

Rykor - the walrus-like alien who is the Mantis Section's top shrink - has just finished wringing information from the little creep who killed the Emperor's favorite Joygirl. It was hard work, and Alex felt that she needed refreshment.

Allan Cole

The Joke:

Alex went to Rykor's tank and looked properly respectful. "Lass, since y' no drinkit, Ah dinnae ken wha' y' should have as ae reward.

"Perhaps a wee fi sh?"

Rykor heaved, flippers coming out of the tank and smashing down, salt water cascading over the room.

For a moment Sten thought she was in convulsions.

"Sergeant Kilgour!" Rykor finally managed as the waves subsided, "and for all these years I felt you humans lacked humor. You are a good man."

"Alex," Sten crooned as he walked over and draped an arm around his sergeant. "At last we've found someone who understands your jokes.

"Your next assignment will be as a walrus."

*****

From The Alex KilgourToxic Scrapheap

Alex surveyed his team and decided they needed a little cheering up.

He said, "A man was waitin' fur his guidwife tae gie birth. Th' doctur cam an' informed th' dad 'at his son was born withit a torso, arms, ur legs. Th' son was jist a heed!

But th' dad loo'd his son an' raised heem an aw as he could. Eighteen years later, th' son was auld enaw fur his first narcobeer. Th' dad took heem tae a pub, tearfully tauld heem he was prood ay heem, an' ordered th' biggest, strongest narcobeer fur his son.

37

Allan Cole

Wi' aw th' bar patrons lookin' oan curioosly, th' son took his first sip and... Swoooop! a torso popped out!

The bar was deid silent, 'en burst intae a whoop ay joy. Th' faither, shocked, begged his son tae drink again. Th' patrons chanted, "Drink anither bevvy! Drink anither bevvy!"

Th' bartender shook his heed in dismay. But th'n - Swoooop! Two arms popped out! The bar went wild. Th' faither, greetin' an' wailin', begged his son tae drink again.

Th' patrons chanted, "Drink anither bevvy! Drink anither bevvy!"

But th' bartender ignored th' whole affair.

By thes time, th' son was gettin' tipsy. Wi' his new hans, he reached doon, grabbed th' narcobeer, an' guzzled th' lest ay it.

N' swoooop! Tois legs popped out!

The bar was a-shout. Th' faither grat wi' joy.

Th' son stuid up oan his new legs. He stumbled tae th' left. He stumbled tae th' reit.

'En he stumbled ben th' front duir an' intae th' causey, whaur a truck ran heem ower.

The bar feel silent.

Th' faither moaned wi' grief.

Th' bartender merely sighed an' said, "He shoods hae quit while he was a heed."

Allan Cole

STEN 4 - Fleet Of The Damned

The Book:

Sten's luck seems to have deserted him. Having been assigned a tacdivision in the Fringe Worlds, he soon discovers that the Imperial Officers are more interested in having fun than honing their fighting skills. The enemy Tahn couldn't have picked a better time or place to launch their long–planned attack against the Empire. Sten and his men are outgunned and outmanned... But Sten isn't going to give up without a fight.

*****

The Setup:

In the previous book, Court Of A Thousand Suns, just about everything went wrong that could go wrong. The Eternal Emperor was rescued, to be sure, but his diplomatic Tahn guests were not. Now, the Empire is at war with the dreaded Tahn. Sten and Alex wind up in the Imperial Navy running a fleet of futuristic PT-Type spacecraft. As things go from bad to worse, Alex attempts to tell the dreaded "Spotted Snakes" story.

The Joke:

Alex leaned closer to him to whisper. "Ah could warm 'em up, if ya like, lad. Tell 'em a wee joke or three."

"No jokes," Sten said firmly.

Alex's response was immediate gloom."No' even the one about the spotted snakes? Tha's perfect for a braw crew such as this."

"You will especially avoid the one about the spotted snakes. Kilgour, there are laws about cruel and unusual punishment. And if you even dream spotted snakes, I'll have you keelhauled."

*****

(Later - The Second Spotted Snake Attempt)

"They'll have eaten all the food by the time we get there," Foss said. Then he remembered himself. "Begging your pardon, sir."

"What other choice do we have?"

"Ah could alw'ys tell tha spotted snake story," Kilgour offered. "Just ta keep our spirits up, like."

(Once again, Sten puts the Kabosh on the joke. But, later on...)

"Puir lad," Alex sympathized. "It's aye the pressure cooker a' command. T' be't so young an' so brainburned."

"You have a better idea?"

"Ah do. An evil plan. Worthy ae a Campbell. Best ae all, it means we dinnae e'en hae't' be around't' be causin't braw death an' destruction."

"GA."

"If y' buy't, can Ah tell the lads ae th' wee spotted snakes?"

"Not even if your plot'll win the war single-handed.

(Still Later: Another try...)

Allan Cole

"I'm not running a combat unit," Sten groaned. "This is a clottin' divinity school!"

"Puir tyke," Alex sympathized. "Next he'll be thinkin't tha be rules a' war. P'raps it'd cheer y' lad, if Ah told th' story ae th' spotted snakes again."

Sten grinned. "I'd keelhaul you, Alex. If I had a keel.

(The Spotted Snake story is averted yet again... but will it return? Not until after the head fake below...And even then the spotted snake doesn't fall until another book!)

*****

The Setup:

Sten, Alex and the other members of the crew are left afoot, up to their arses in clotting snow. As their spirits flag, Alex decides that as self-appointed Morale Officer, he must step in.

The Joke:

... Sten had to threaten him with close arrest to keep him from telling the awesomely imbecilic spotted snake story—Sten had heard it once back during Mantis training—three times too many.

Kilgour had other stories that were almost as bad.

"Ha' Ah gie y' aboot in' time Ah were tourin't th' estate," he began cheerily to Ensign Tapia.

"What's an estate?" she growled as she almost fell face first into a drift.

Allan Cole

"Ah, wee Sten, pardon, Commander Sten, hae dinnae spoke th' Ah'm th' rightful Laird Kilgour ae Kilgour?"

"I have no idea what you're talking about."

"Ah'm tryin't't' tell y' boot th' pig."

"Pig?"

"Aye. A great mound ae swineflesh, ae were. A' any rate, th' first Ah e'er saw ae tha' pig wae when Ah wa' tourin't th' estate. An' Ah seeit thae great porker. An' it strikit me, for it hae a wooden leg. Three legs an' aye, a peg."

"A three-legged pig," Foss put in suspiciously, having waded up close enough to Tapia to hear the story.

"Aye. A wonderment. So thae's this wee farmer standin't nigh his fence. An' I begin't an say, "Tha' pig, mister...'

"An' he speakit, an say, 'Aye, aye. Thae's a pig ae marvel. Three year ago, m' wee lad fall't down. Inta th' pond. Tha' dinnae be anyone around, an' m' heir's a drown't.

"'Doon plung't th' pig, an' pull him out.'

"An' Ah'm listen't, an' Ah say't, 'Tha's ae marvel. But—'

"An once't 'gain he cuts me off. 'Two year gone, m' gran's in th' gravsled, an' the controls go. An' the gravsled lifts an' 'tis headed for yon viaduct.'"

"Viaduct?" Tapia asked.

"Noo, tha's a fair question, lass. Ah'll answer in a bit. T' continue. I agree wi' m' wee tenant. 'Aye, tha's a pig tha's a wonder. But about'... an' ag'in he chops me.

"'One year past, 'tis a deep winter. Y' c'lect, Laird Kilgour.' An Ah says, 'Aye, Ah remember.'

Allan Cole

"An he says, 'M' croft catches fire. An' we're all asleep ae' th' dead. But this pig, he storm't ae th' hoose an' wakit us all. Savin't our lives.'

"Ae tha' point, Ah hae enough. 'Be holdin't tha' speech, man,' Ah roars. 'Ah 'gree. 'Tis a marvelous hog. Wha' Ah want to know is, Why th' clottin' wooden leg!?'

"An th' crofter look't ae me, an' say, 'Why, mon, you dinnae eat ae pig like thae all at once!'"

Tapia and Foss, both thinking indictable thoughts about premeditated murder, continued wading through the snow.

That was Alex on the march.

*****

From The Alex Kilgour Toxic Scrapheap

The Setup:

During a narcobeer break, the crew members are bragging on the military exploits of their parents. The stories get grander and grander, until Alex can bear no more. He orders another round, then tells this tale.

The Joke:

"When Ah was jist a wee laddie mah teacher gae us all a class assignment:'G ie uir parents tae teel a story wi' a moral at th' end ay it,' she say.

Allan Cole

"Th' next day th' bairns cam back an' a body by a body began tae teel their stories. Finally, Ah was th' only a body left. Ain th' teacher says, 'Alex, dae ye hae a story tae shaur?'"

"'Aye, mum,'" Ah say. 'Mah mother tauld a story abit mah Aunt Annis. She was a fighter pilot in th' Mueller wars an' one body day 'er ship was burst by th' enemy.

"She hud tae bail it ower enemy territory an' all she hud was a flask ay whiskey, a willygun an' a sharp chib. So, mah Aunt Annis drenk th' whiskey oan th' way doon sae it woods nae break.

"'An' then 'er parachute landed reit in th' middle ay twintie enemy troaps.

"She shot fifteen ay them wi' th' willygun, until th' power went dry. Killed fower mair wi' th' chib, 'till th' blade broke. An' 'en she killed th' lest cheil wi' 'er baur hans.'"

"Aye, that's wha I told the class, but my teacher was shocked at th' tale. 'My goodness," she said. 'What kin' ay moral did yer mum teel ye frae 'at gantin' story?'

"So Ah tauld her: 'Stay th' clot awa' frae Aunt Annis when she's bin drinkin'!"

Allan Cole

STEN 5 - Revenge Of The Damned

The Book:

Sten had fully expected to die in a blaze of glory, taking the Emperor's greatest foe with him. Instead, he ended up a slave laborer in a POW camp deep in the heart of enemy territory. But sitting out the action had never been Sten's style. And now that the war was building to a climax, the Eternal Emperor needed him more than ever. Not even the toughest prison in the known universe can keep Sten from his mission…

*****

The Setup:

Captured by the Tahn, Sten and Alex are stuck in a Tahn camp, supposedly impossible to escape from. (Think: The Great Escape) Naturally, they immediately start planning an elaborate escape - breaking out half the prison if they can. Alex finds a moment when he thinks his fellow beings need cheering up. His medicine - Oh, no, The Spotted Snake story.)

The Joke:

"... While we be hain't ae sec," Alex said, "whidny y' be likin't Ae tellin't th' aboot th' spotted snakes?"

Sten glared. "If you do that, I shall assassinate you."

"Th' lad hae nae sense a' humor," Alex complained to the sleeping reek in the tiny box in front of them.

*****

(Once again, Alex's mates - and our loyal readers - are saved from the spotted snake story. But, not for long! Watch what happens when Sten and Alex try to suborn a Tahn guard and Alex goes for broke!)

Spotted Snakes Redux:

"I wouldn't want to be a POW," N'chlos said firmly.

"True. An' thae's nae th' worst thae can happen." Kilgour paused. "E'en when y'hae no fightin't, thae's little joy. F'r instance, dinnae Ah tell you ae the spotted snakes?"

"I don't think so." Kilgour spared a minismile for Sten, and Sten glowered back. The clot had trapped him, well and truly. "I was ae Earth. Ae a wee isle called Borneo."

"You've been to Earth!" N'chlos was astonished.

"Aye, lad. Th' service broadin't thae background. At any rate, an't' go on, Ah'd jus' taken' o'er a wee detachment ae troops."

"I didn't know Imperial warrant officers did that."

"Special circumstances," Alex went on. "An' so Ah calls th' sarn't major in, an Ah asks, 'Sarn't Major, whae's thae worst problem?'

"An' he say't, 'Spotted snakes!'

"An' Ah says, 'Spotted snakes?'

"An' he says, 'Spotted snakes, sir.'"

Allan Cole

At that point the cell door opened silently, and an arm—St. Clair's arm—snaked in. Her hand lifted N'chlos's tunic off the peg, and tunic and arm vanished.

"Here's th' caff, sir. Anyhoot, Ah'm looki't ae th' fiche on m' new unit, an' it's awful. Thae's desertion, thae's a crime sheet thae long, thae's social diseases up th' gumpstump—m' command's a wreck!

"So, Ah call't th' unit' t'gether an' questions m' men on whae's th' problem. "An' they chorus, 'Ae's th' spotted snakes, sir.'

" 'Spotted snakes?' Ah asks.

"'Aye, sir. Spotted snakes,' they chorus.

"An' thae explain't thae's all these spotted snakes in th' jungle. Ah did say th' detachment wae in th' center ae a braw jungle, dinnae Ah?"

Outside, Sten hoped, N'chlos's tunic was being searched. His soldier book and any other papers were tossed to the prison's fastest runner, who darted downstairs to a cell where L'n waited.

His papers were scrutinized and memorized by her artistically eidetic memory, to be reproduced later.

The tunic was measured, and all uniform buttons had wax impressions made, also for reproduction. The stun rod's measurements were taken just in case someone needed to build a phony weapon.

Within minutes the escape committee would have all the essentials on the off chance that an escaper might want or need to look like a guard. Or maybe to use N'chlos as a cover identity.

Allan Cole

Unless, of course, N'chlos turned around, realized his uniform was missing, and shouted an alert.

But in the meantime Sten squirmed under Alex's story.

"An' aye," Kilgour went on. "Thae wee spotted snakes. All over th' place. Wee fierce lads w' a braw deadly poison. Crawl in th' fightin' positions an' bites, crawl in th' tents an' bites, crawl in the mess an' bites. Awful creatures. Som'at hae be done.

"So Ah considers an' then orders up aye formation. An' comit out, an th' men gasp, seein't Ah'm holdin' a spotted snake.

"An' Ah say, 'Listen't up, men. Ah hae here a spotted snake, aye?'

"An' th' men chorus back, 'Aye sir, ae spotted snake.'

" 'Now, Ah'm goin't't' show you th' solution to thae spotted snakes. Ae's by th' numbers. Wi' th' count ae one, y' securit th' snake wi' your right hand. Wi' th' count ae two, y' secure th' snake wi' your left hand as well. Wi' th' count ae three, y' slid't y'r right hand up't' its wee head, an pop, on th' count ae four, y' snappit th' snake's head off wi' y'r thumb!'

"An' th' men's eyes goggle, an then they go't' war.

"F'r th' next two weeks, thae's all y' hear around th' detachment. Pop…pop…pop…pop. Thae's wee snake heads lyin't all around."An th' morale picks up, an' thae's noo more deserters, an' thae's nae crime sheet, an' e'en the pox rate drops a notch.

"M' problem's solved. An' then, one day, Ah'm visitin' th' dispensary.

Allan Cole

"An' thae's one puir lad lying't thae, an' he's swathed in bandages. Head't' foot. Bandages.

"An' Ah ask't 'Whae happen?'

"An' he croakit, 'Spotted snakes, sir!'

"'Spotted snakes,' Ah says.

"'Aye, sir. Spotted snakes.'

"'G'on lad,' Ah says."

Alex was looking a little worried—then the door opened again, and the same silent arm replaced the tunic and weapons belt. Alex hesitated, then put his story—if that was what it was—back on track. Sten was trying to remember just what the most painful and slowest method of execution he knew of was and was determined to apply it to his warrant officer.

"'Sir,' th' lad in bandages goes on. 'Y' know how y' told us how't' deal wi' th' spotted snakes?'

" 'Aye, spotted snakes. But Ah dinnae ken—'

" 'Ah'm tryin't't' tell you. Ah'm in m' fightin' position ae stand-to th' other night. An' thae wee furrit object wi' spots slides in m' hole. An' just like y' ordered, Mr. Kilgour, on th' count ae one Ah grabs it wi' m' right hand, on th' count ae two Ah grabs it wi' m' left hand, on th' count ae three Ah slides m' hand up, an' on th' count ae four Ah pop… an' sü, can y' fancy m' sittin' thae wi' m' thumb up a tiger's arse?'"

There was dead, complete silence.

Finally N'chlos spoke. "That is the worst clotting joke I have ever heard."

Allan Cole

And for the first and only time, Sten found himself in complete agreement with a Tahn.

*****

The Setup:

The Spotted Snake story out of the way, Alex proceeds to "help" Sten charm a cunning lady thief that our hero has less than honorable designs on. The beauty's name is St. Clair.

The Joke:

"Lately I don't feel like we're getting anywhere. We're wrecking their money. Fine and good. We're fouling up production. Messing with their morale. Stealing their secrets. And being a general pain in the tush. This is great. As it should be. We're hurting them bad."

"I don't see what your problem is," L'n said. "What more do you want?"

"I want to hear them yell ouch," St. Clair said. "I mean, how bad are we really hurting them?"

"Aye," Alex said, tapping the table thoughtfully. "Ah ken whae y' mean."

"You do?" asked the unsuspecting L'n, who still had a few innocent bits left in her.

Alex nodded wisely. " Tis ae old malady," he said. "How much hurt hurts. Aye. An old tale, lass. Let Kilgour tell y' how old."

And Alex settled back to tell a suspicious St. Clair and an intrigued L'n his story.

50

Allan Cole

"Ae gran'sire ae mine wae trappin't. Ae Eart'. Bleakit an' cold an' a'. Been oot ae th' wilderness aye weeks an' months.

"An' one day, thae was a wee town. Nae, no e'en a town. A village. Thae see't thae great pourit ae snow comin't toward them. An' thae thinki't ae's a bear or some'at.

"M' grandsire, 'twere.

"Lookin't f'r ae dentist.

"Turns oot, thae's a diploma-mill quack ae thae village. An' m' gran'sire sits doon ae th' chair, an' thae dentist lookit ae' his teeth an' say, 'Aye, thae's got to coom oot. But ae nae hae anesthesia.'

"M' grandsire say, 'Dinnae fash. Pull it.'

"An so, wi' great gruntin' ae groanin't, thae dentist yankit thae tooth. An' he's sweatin', an m' grandsire's sweatin't.

"An' thae quack say't, 'Dinnae thae be th' greatest pain y've ever felt?'

"M' grandsire says, 'Nae. Thae's naught.'

"Wi' considerable astonishment, thae dentist say, 'Whae's worse?'

"M' grandsire, explain't. 'Last week, Ah come down wi' th' runs. S' bad, Ah canne mak't oot m' cabin't' thae backhouse. So, Ah drap m' trews ae th' snowbank, right outside m' door. An' Ah forget Ah was cleanin't m' bear traps before thae snow fell, an' Ah left a wee trap set right where't Ah be crouchin't.

" 'Which Ah'm remindit aboot when thae trap closit.

" 'Snapit closit on m' balls.'

51

Allan Cole

" 'Good Lord,' thae dentist sae. 'Y'r right. Thae's th' biggest pain ae all.'

" 'Nae, nae, lad,' m' grandsire say. 'Th' biggest pain ae all wae when Ah come to the end ae th' chain...' "

His punch line was greeted by the usual cold, stony silence. But only from St. Clair. L'n was on the floor with laughter. Alex gave her a huge, fond smile.

"I don't get it," St. Clair said flatly.

"You—you don't?" L'n gasped through laughter. "Why not? It's—so simple that it's—" She broke off to compose herself. "Look. A bear trap has this big long chain."

"I know that," St. Clair said, a little miffed.

"And one end of the chain is staked to the ground. And on the other end is—well, the bear trap. And, see, when the jaws snapped shut, they caught Alex's great-great-whatever-grand-father by the scrotum."

She erupted into laughter again. St. Clair just glared at her. Alex thought she was absolutely wonderful.

"But—see, that still wasn't what really hurt the most," L'n went on. "What really hurt was-"

"I don't want to hear it again," St. Clair broke in. "Please!"

Alex got to his feet and strode around the table to L'n. He patted her fondly on the shoulder. She was a being after his own heart. Kilgour had found himself a duck.

"Do you know any more like that?" L'n asked hopefully.

"A few, lass. Just a few. D'ya e'er ken thae one aboot th' spotted snake?"

Allan Cole

"Nooo… I don't think so. Why don't you—"

"Don't get him started, L'n," Sten's voice boomed from across the room. "Or you'll wish you were back in a Koldyeze cooler."

*****

The Setup:

In a change of pace, this shaggy dog story is told by Chetwynd, a character we met in Court Of A Thousand Suns. There, he was the tough boss prisoner of a colony of convicts. Somehow he escaped. Now he's on a Tahn world finds himself joining forces with Sten and Alex against a common enemy. (Sidenote: The character was named for Lionel Chetwynd, an old friend and a damned good writer. Check him out at IMBD.com)

The Joke:

Chetwynd put on a brave leader face and entered.

He bought a round for his boyos.

He sipped the shot he wanted to slug down.

He held court, awarded and withheld approval, granted or withheld favors—and told the latest Tahn joke:

"A mister finally gets the vid. He's on the list. Through priorities. His gravsled is fin'ly available.

"He goes bug. 'Bout time. Paid the Tahn guv for it six years ago. When is he gonna get it?

"Tahn motorpool clot says four years down. Whitsl-cycle. Fourth day.

"Mister asks that be in the morning or afternoon?

Allan Cole

"Tahn clerk says, 'Mister, that be four years away! Why do you care if it's morning or night?'

" 'Cause I got the plumber coming in the morning.'

During the laughter he blasted down the rest of the shot and waved for another.

*****

From The Alex Kilgour Toxic Scrapheap

The Setup:

Here's another told by Chetwynd, except we had to cut it for space.

The Joke:

A prisoner escapes from one of the worst prisons in the whole clottin' Empire. On the run, he comes across a likely house breaks into it. To his delight he finds a young couple in bed. He gets the guy out of the bed, ties him up on a chair, ties the woman to the bed and while he's checking her bonds he leans down and kisses her on the neck. Then he gets up, and goes to the bathroom.

While he's in there, the husband tells his wife: "Listen, this guy is a prisoner, look at his clothes! He probably spent a lot of time in prison, and has not seen a woman in years. I saw the way he kissed your neck. If he wants sex, don't resist, don't complain, just do what he tells you, give him satisfaction. This guy must be dangerous, if he gets angry, he will kill us. Be strong, honey. I love you!"

54

Allan Cole

The wife smiles sweetly and replies, "I am glad you think that way, dear. I'm sureyou are right - he hasn't seen a woman in years.

"But, honey, he was not kissing my neck. He was whispering in my ear. He told me that he found you very sexy, and asked if we kept any Vaseline in the bathroom...

"Be strong honey. I love you too..."

*****

The Setup:

This story was told by the real Alex Kilgour, who was reminiscing about the "good old days," and we later adapted it for Revenge Of The Damned. We envisioned it like this: Alex and the other POW tunnel rats are taking a much-deserved break. They'd been digging for clottin' weeks and yet it seemed they'd made depressingly little progress. In his never ending quest to improve morale, Alex pops out with this:

The Joke:

"A sodger fa jist enlisted speart th' master sergeant fur a three-day pass. The master sergeant gawped, 'Aur ye a bampot? Yoo jist join th' Imperial army, an' ye awreddy want a pass? Sodger, fur 'at kin' ay a reward ye hae tae dae somethin' bonnie clottin' spectacular!'

"A day later th' sodger returned in a huge enemy grav-track! The master sergeant was clottin' bloon awa'.

"He speart 'Haw did ye dae it?'

The sodger replied, "Weel, Ah jumped in a body ay uir grav-tracks, an' went toward th' border wi' th' enemy. As Ah got near,

55

Allan Cole

Ah saw an enemy track. Ah pit mah white flag up, an' th' enemy track pit his white flag up.

"'An' Ah said tae th' enemy sodger, 'Do ye want tae gie a three-day pass? Sae we exchanged tracks."

(Aren't you sorry we didn't have room for that one?)

*****

The Setup:

This little tidbit was to be told by St. Clair, the beautiful conwoman enlisted by Sten to be the Tahn POW Camp's scrounger.

The Joke:

"The first man and woman in Creation just had to be citizens of Tahn. I mean, here we have Adam and Eve believing they were in Paradise when all along they were homeless, naked and only had one apple between them."

*****

The Setup:

This Kilgour story made it all the way to the next to the last draft, where it was cut. It's told during their elaborate efforts to escape the Tahn POW camp.

The Joke:

"Aye, here's a tale mah auld grain faither tauld me. He said in ancient times thaur was a stoatin war oan Planit Earth, an' ye ken if th' Kilgoors sniff a war, they cannae help but join in.

Allan Cole

"Mah auld ancestur - Captain Kilgoor - ended up bein' a pilot fightin' a coontry ay men waur e'en than even th' Tahn. Nazis, they waur called.

Anyhaw, Captain Kilgour's plane was brooght doon an' he's captured by th' Nazis, who w're more cruel th'n the Tahn. He was was sorely woonded, an' a body day when a Nazi doctur tauld heem, "Scotsman! yer arm is infected wi' gangrene we main cut it aff."

"Oh, aye, mah ancestur didne loch thes bark at aw. but he was brae, sae he said, 'Okay, 'en. but coods ye drap it ower Scootlund when ye gang bombin' them?'

"The Nazi laughed an' said, "h, we will be canty tae.'

"A few weeks later th' Nazi doctur tauld Captain Kilgoor 'at they hae tae cut aff his other arm. Sae mah ancestur, he says, 'Okay, 'en. But coods drap it ower Scootlund loch ye did lest time?'

"'Yes, 'at will be dain,' said th' Nazi.

Later, th' Nazi tells Captain kilgoor 'at they hae tae cut his leg aff. Ance again mah brae th' ancestur says, 'Weel, coods ye dae th' sam as afair?'

"The Nazi replies, 'Och aye."

The next th' Nazi tells heem they hae tae cut his other leg. 'Weel,' begins Captain Kilgoor, 'coods ye jist...'

But the Nazi shooted most sevaur. "No! It wulnae be dain. We ken yer clever plan! Ye ur tryin' tae escape tae scootlund!"

Allan Cole

STEN 6 - Return Of The Emperor

The Book:

The Eternal Emperor was dead, and the five members of the Privy Council ruled in his place. But they quickly discovered that their power would collapse around them if they didn't locate the Emperor's secret source of Anti–Matter Two, the economic keystone of the Empire. And so they sent a team of crack commandos to capture Sten, one of their late ruler's few surviving confidantes. But Sten, as usual, had his own agenda. For he knew something about the Eternal Emperor that would shake the Empire to its foundations. And to play his part, all Sten had to do was kill the five most powerful beings in the universe…

*****

The Setup:

The previous book - Revenge Of The Damned - ended with another Bunch & Cole trademark cliffhanger: the assassination of the Eternal Emperor. Legend has it that he's been assassinated before, but always came back. Will he this time? Well, Duh! Meanwhile, the evil corporate leaders (are there any other kind) who form The Privy Council are hunting down Sten and Alex, believing that they possess the secret of where in clot the Emperor kept the AM2 - the fuel that powered the Empire.

The Joke:

Laird Kilgour of Kilgour, formerly Chief Warrant Officer Alex Kilgour (First Imperial Guards Division, Retired); formerly CWO A. Kilgour, Detached, Imperial Service, Special Duties; formerly Private-through-Sergeant Kilgour, Mantis Section Operational, various duties from demolitions expert to sniper to clandestine training, to include any duties the late Eternal Emperor wanted performed sub rosa with a maximum of lethality, was holding forth.

"... An' aye, th' rain's peltin' doon, f'r days an' days i' comes doon. An' her neighbors tell th' li'l old gran, 'Bes' y' flee't' high ground.'

" 'Nae,' she says. 'Ah hae faith. God will take care a' me. Th' Laird wi' provide.' "

It was a beautiful evening. The tubby man was sprawled on a settee, his feet on a hassock, his kilt tucked decorously between his legs. Conveniently to his right were his weapons of choice: a full pewter flagon of Old Sheepdip, imported at staggering—staggering to anyone not as rich as Kilgour—expense from Earth and a liter mug of lager.

(Alex is interrupted, but later continues stubbornly onward.)

*****

Allan Cole

An th' rain comit doon an' comit doon, an' th' water's risin'. And her pigs are wash't away, squealin't. An' the' coo's swimmin't f'r shelter. An doon th' road comit ae gravcar.

" 'Mum,' comit th' shout. 'Thae's floodin't. Thae must leave!' " 'Nae,' she shouts back. 'Ah'll noo leave. Th' Laird will provide.'

"An' th' water comit up, an' comit up, an' th' rain i' pel tin' an comit doon. An' the chickens ae roostin' ae the roof. Floodin't her house't' ae th' first story. An' here comit ae boat. 'Missus, now thae must leave. We'll save y'!'

"An' agin comit her answer: 'Nae, nae. Th' Laird will provide.'

"But th' rain keep fallin't. An' th' water keep't risin't. An' coverin't th' second story. An' she's crouchin' ae th' roof, wi' th' chickens, an' here comit ae rescue gravlighter. It hover't o'er th' roof, an' a mon leans oot. 'Mum! We're here't'save y'.'

"But still she's steadfast. Once again, 'Nae, nae. Th' Laird will provide.'

"An' th' rain keep fallin't an' th' flood keep't risin't. An' she drowns. Dead an' a'.

"An' she goes oop't' Heaven. An' th' Laird's waitin'. An' th' wee gran lady, she's pissed!

"She gets right i' Th' Good Laird's face, an shouts, 'How c'd y', Laird! Th' one time Ah aski't frae help—an ye're nae there.' "

The com buzzed. The guvnor answered. "Alex. F'r you. From your hotel."

"B'dam," Alex swore. But he rose. "Hold m'point. 'Tis nae a good one, nae a long one, but be holdin't it anyway."

60

Allan Cole

(Once again, Alex's progress is halted. Will this gag ever be clotting over?)

*****

He had a second for a final mourn.

"Nae m'friends'll nae hear the last line:

"An' th' Laird looki't ae her, an' he's sore puzzled. 'Gran, how can y' say Ah dinnae provide?

"Ah giv't ae car, ae boat, an ae gravlighter!'"

*****

From The Alex Kilgour Toxic Scrapheap

The Setup:

None, really. The next three stories were adapted from old Soviet Union jokes told to us by a writer friend who was the son of one of the Hollywood Ten who were blacklisted and jailed during the Red Scare back in the 50's. We wanted to use them in "Return," but never found a good place for them.

Joke #1:

As we all know, the poor Tahn live in constant terror of their government. And just before the outbreak of war with the Empire there were mass arrests across all the planets under their power. People lived in even greater fear, especially at night, expecting to be carted away by the Tahn Socio-Patrolmen.

One night there was a loud knock at the door of a certain house.

61

Allan Cole

The residents cowered in silence, afraid to answer it. The knocking continued, getting louder and louder.

The residents didn't budge - pretending to be asleep. Finally someone started to break down the door.

As he listened to the door give way, one resident thinks to himself: "I'm an old man, I've got to die soon anyway. What am I afraid of? I'll open up to them."

He gets up and goes to the door. A minute later he rushes back to his family, shouting joyfully:

"Get up! Get up! It's only a fire . . .'

*****

Joke #2:

The Tahn Prime Minister read his report to the gathered members of Parliament. Suddenly someone sneezed. "Who sneezed?" (Silence.) "First row! On your feet! Shoot them!" (Applause.) "Who sneezed?" (Silence.) "Second row! On your feet! Shoot them!" (Long, loud applause.) "Who sneezed?" (Silence.) ...A dejected voice in the back: "It was me" (Sobs.) The Tahn Prime Minister leaned forward: "Bless you, Citizen!"

*****

Joke #3

A Tahn judge strolled out of his chambers laughing his head off. A fellow judge approached and asked what was so funny.

The first judge said, "I just heard the funniest joke in the world!"

62

Allan Cole

"Well, go ahead, tell me!" said the other judge.

Still snickering, the first judge said, "I can't. I just sentenced some poor clot to the firing squad for telling it!"

Allan Cole

STEN 7 - Vortex

The Book:

The Empire is in chaos. The once–great Imperial Navy has been shattered in battle and lies burning in space, riven by a civil war that threatens to engulf humanity's future. For the revered Eternal Emperor is not the man his subjects thought him to be — and may not even be human at all. And it is Sten — Imperial bodyguard, spy, assassin, renegade — who now leads humanity's fight for survival. Taking command of the last rebel fleet, he sets out on a desperate quest to seek and destroy the dark source of his former master's power. Denounced as a traitor, hunted by forces loyal to the Emperor, Sten must risk everything to annihilate the Empire he vowed to protect.

The Setup:

The Eternal Emperor returned after all, but all is not well. He's behaving very strangely indeed. No longer the benevolent dictator we've learned to love. Meanwhile, a planetary system inhabited by several very nasty breeds of beings - all hating each other's guts - are disrupting the Empire. (Think: the breakup of Yugoslavia, or the U.S.S.R.) Sten is sent as Plenipotentiary to solve the problem. Alex, naturally enough, is at his side. In the opening, Sten is getting orders from his old boss and buddy, Ian Mahoney,

The Scene:

Mahoney laughed. Sten, more than familiar with situations when sudden merriment sans joke were required, also laughed.

"Fine, Ian. If we're telling old stinkers, here's one of Kilgour's. After all these years I'm even getting pretty good with his dialect."

As his mouth began the words to the half-remembered joke, Sten forbade himself a guilty look back over his shoulder at Arundel Castle... and concentrated on jokes, obscene, Scots, stupid.

The Joke:

"Hae Ah e'er told y' ae th' time Ah entered a limerick contest? Y' ken whae lim'ricks are, aye?"

"We're not totally uncivilized."

"Thae's bonnie. Twas whae Ah was a wee striplin't, assigned t' a honor guard on Earth. Th' tabs announc'd thae contest. Large credits f r th' prize. Who c'd come up wi' thae dirtiest, filthiest, lim'rick?

"Well, Ah hae braw experience when it com ft' dirty, filthy lim'ricks."

"I've never questioned that."

Allan Cole

"Ah'm payin't nae heed nor reck f thae cheap one, Major. So Ah ship't m' filthy poem away, an aye, 'twas so filthy e'en a striplin't like m'self blushed a bit, thinkin't m' name wae attach't.

"But thae credits wae bonny, as Ah've said. An' lord know't a puir wee ranker needs a' th' coin he can secure. So time pass't an' time pass't, an' then one day Ah sees th' tab, an' Ah'm thunderstrick!

"Ah'm noo th' winner! Ah hae nothin'! Th' winner's some clot nam'd McGuire. D. M. McGuire, ae' th' wee isle ae Eire, they name't it, frae th' city ae Dublin. An' th' lim'rick's so dirty thae cannae e'en run thae own prizewinner!

"An a'ter Ah recover frae m' heartbroke, it starts gnawin't ae me. I mean, thae cannae be a filthier lim'rick thae whae Ah submitt'd.

"So Ah taki't a wee bit ae leave, an Ah moseys t' Eire, an' thae cap'tal ae Dublin, an' Ah begins lookin't frae D. M. McGuire. Days an' weeks pass, aye, but finally Ah trackit doon th' last McGuire i' Dublin.

"She's a wee gran lady. Sweet, wi' a twinkle i' her eye, an' a smile ae her lips, an' y' jus' know she's goin ft' church ever' day, twice't, an' thae's nae been a foul word cross her lips.

"This cannae be th' D. M. McGuire ae the contest, but Ah'm des'prate. So I screws m' courage t' th' stickity point, an' asks.

"Dam't near crap m' kilt, when she says, 'Aye. Ah am.' "Ah begs her f'r whae it was.

"I's noo her turn t' blush, an' she say't 'Ah'm a respect'ble widow. Ah cannae use language like thae around a man.'

Allan Cole

"She talk't funny, she did. 'Twae hard f' me t' understand her, sometime.

"Ah ask't her to write it doon, e'en. But she cannae do thae, e'er. Thae must be the scummiest poem e'er wrote. So Ah argue, an' argue, an' plea, an' finally she say't, 'Cannae Ah tell it, but wi' blankety frae th' vile words?'

"A course, Ah says. AMI hae nae grief figurin't it oot frae there. "An' she tak't ae deep breath, an' recites:

> "Blankety-blankety blank
> Blankety-blankety blank
> Blankety-blank
> Blankety-blank
> Blankety river of shit."

After a long silence... a giggle. Alex beamed. "Ah knoo frae th' first thae wae someat aboot y' Ah admired. Noo thae's three."

*****

From The Alex Kilgour Toxic Scrapheap

The Background:

When this joke was told to us Chris and I were on the floor. We tucked it aside for a definite Kilgour joke candidate. But when the time came we disagreed on whether it should go in. Chris thought it was a great joke, but only as a Visual joke. In other words, you had to see the punch line acted out to get the joke. I disagreed. The way we worked the writing partnership was that in any disagreement, the one who did the disagreeing

67

Allan Cole

got an automatic 51% vote. Don't laugh. It worked for nearly twenty years. Anyway, here's Cole's Revenge. You be the judge.

The Setup:

Kilgour is appalled - but not surprised - at how much hate is being spewed by warring beings throughout the star-cluster. He tells Sten and Cind that it reminds him of the rivalries he's read about in ancient times, and how one group was always trying to outdo the other, no matter what the circumstances. We didn't get this one in Vortex as planned, but I still think Alex makes a most excellent point.

The Joke:

Three men - an Englishman, a Frenchman an' a bonny Scotsman - crash lain oan a desert islain. In a clottin' flash, they ur captured by savages an' dragged tae th' village camp.

A tall, handsome Chieftain comes out ay a hut an' strides up tae them.

'Gentlemen,' he says. 'I am th' chieftain ay thes tribe.'

"The men ur surprised at his cultured speech an' looks. Th' yoong chieftain laughs at their reactions an' says, "Oh, Ah ken 'at we swatch loch savages haur, An' Ah suppose we ur. An', as ye nae doobt feared, we ur cannibals too.

"The thee men swatch at th' huge cookin' pot steamin' an' boilin' ower a fire in th' center ay th' village. They blanche, afeared.

Allan Cole

"The chieftain speaks mair soothingly, noo. 'We main be savages, but we arenae barbarians,' he says. 'Fur example, Ah was educated at th' finest university oan prime warld. But, returned tae spreid whit wee wisdom civilization has tae offer.'

"The thee men ur silent, tryin' tae pit up a brae front. But, they dreid whit is tae come. The yoong chieftain says, 'We ur much closer tae nature than ye. Mair pure, Ah hink.

"'Oh, we will takes yer li'es, 'at is fur certain. But tak' comfort in th' fact 'at nae a body hin' frae yer body will be wasted. We will eat yer flesh, ay coorse. But, also, we will use yer anes fur tools.

"'An' we'll use yer skin as well. We will stretch an' dry yer skins an' make them intae marveloos canoes.'

"Sstill th' men say naethin'. Then th' yoong chieftain draws a huge knife frae his belt.

"'Ain tae prove tae ye further 'at we arenae savages, we will gie ye th' choice ay takin' yer ain li'es - in sic' a way 'at will shaw yer coorage - yer manliness.'

"The Frenchman's bonds ur loosened an' th' chieftain hans heem th' sharp chib. Immediately, th' Frenchman raises th' chib an' shoots, 'Viva la France!' An' he plunges th' chib intae his chest an' collapses, deid. Th' nati'es drag heem tae th' fire an' jobby his body intae th' pot.

The Englishman is next, an' vowin' nae tae be ootdain by th' Frenchman, he raises th' chib high, shootin', 'God Sae Th' Queen' An' he dri'es th' knife deep intae his heart. His body is throon intae th' pot as weel.

Allan Cole

Finally, it is th' scotsman's turn. He has bin watchin' aw thes an' thinkin' oan aw th' yoong chieftain has said. So, he rises tae his foo heecht. raises th' chib oan high...

...Then begins tae stab himself aw ower his body, shoutin', Clot yer canoe! clot yer canoe! Clot yer canoe!'"

Allan Cole

STEN 8 - Empire's End

The Book:

At last! The explosive finale of Sten's adventures as the Eternal Emperor's most trusted friend, bodyguard, troubleshooter...and assassin! See Sten undertake the ultimate treasure hunt, as he and his comrades seek out the source of the Eternal Emperor's power: Anti-Matter Two. Learn the secret of the Eternal Emperor's past: Who is he? Where did he come from? And how did he become immortal? Watch as the loyal Sten turns traitor at last, turning on the Eternal Emperor to save his own skin...and the Empire itself! Eternity is doomed to end. And if Sten has his way, it will end sooner than later!

The Setup:

The Eternal Emperor has gone around the bend. Mad as the proverbial mercury-soaked hatter. He's decided Sten is his worst enemy and is hunting him down with everything he's got. Sten, naturally, only runs so far. Then turns back to take on history's mightiest ruler. As always, Alex is at his side to slay bad guys, run the crew, and lighten the mood when all the world is going to drakh.

The Joke:

Are y' religious, lass?"

"Nossir. But my crèche was."

"Then th' fable be e'en closer't' y'r heart. Seems thae was a man. Nae a puir man, nae a laird. But he's livin't i' a wee house, an' he dinnae like it, but he canna fin' th' money frae a bigger one.

"So he hears aboot a wise man. Ver', ver' wise, he is. An he determines't' consult thae' wise man.

"Bein't wise, a' course it's a't'rble journey't' find him. But eventually our hero climbs't' th' top ae th' mountain where th' magi hangi't his beanie, an' he pleads, 'Great One, what c'n Ah do? M' house i' wee an' Ah canna stand it.'

"Th' wise man thinks, an' asks, 'Hae y' a coo?'

" 'A coo?'

" 'Aye, a coo."

" 'Aye, Ah hae a braw Hereford.'

" 'Move it i' y'r house.'

"An' th' wise man refus't't' say more, i' spite ae th' man's pleadin't an' cryin't. So th' man goes back home, an' aye, it's e'en more a't'rble trek.

"An' he's thinkit, an wonderin't, but he knows th' wise man's truly wise, an' so he moves his coo in't' sleep wi' him. An' his wee house is e'en wee-er.

"An' he canna stand it. So he goes back, 't'rble journey thae it is, all th' way't' th' wise man, an' again asks th' question.

"Th' wise man thinks, an' then he says, 'Hae y' a goat?'

Allan Cole

" 'A goat?'

" 'Aye, a goat.'

" 'Ah hae a goat.'

"Move it i' th' house, too.'

"An' once again, th' wise man refuse't say more.

"So th' man, noo puzzled sorely, wander't back't' his wee home, an' thinkit. But 'cause th' sage i' truly wise, he move th' goat i' wi' him an' th' coo."An' noo he truly canna stand it, f'r his house is e'en smaller."

So again, he goes back't' th' wise man, an' asks f'r help, sayin't 'Ah hae a wee house, noo wi' a coo an' a goat i' it, an' i's bleedin' crowded, an' Ah canna stand it.'

"An' th' wise man think't, an' then he says, 'Hae y' chickens?' 'Chickens?' 'Aye, chickens.' 'Aye, Ah hae chickens.'

" 'Move 'em i' th' house. Come't' ponder, i' y' hae ducks, an' swans, an' pigs, hae them i' the house ae well.'

"An' despite th' man's pleadin', th' wise man sayit noo more.

"But th' man goes back home, an' puts th' chickens in th' house. An' noo i's worse, i's so bad i's intolerable. Thae's no room left i' th' house f'r th' man, i's so crowded.

"An' he journeys back yet again't' th' wise man, an' says, 'Ah canna stand it! M' wee house hae naught but animals i' it, an' there's noo room ae all f'r me! Noo, Ah'm pleadin't, help me!'

"An' th' wise man sayit, 'Go home, an' take all th' animals oot ae th' house.'

Allan Cole

"An' thae's all he'll say.

"An' th' man rush't home, an' clear oot all th' animals, an' y' ken whae he discovered? He still hae a wee house. But noo it's entire full ae animal shit!"

*****

The Setup:

It's near the end of the book - and the series. Sten is being pressured to take the throne that the Eternal Emperor was forced to vacate - fatally, and by Sten. As always, Alex has more than a few words of wisdom to add to the mix.

The Joke:

"I just wonder," Sten said, "if anybody ever knows when that time is? Or," he said, being as honest as he knew how, "if every time somebody gets offered a crown, he always thinks that he's taking it just for universal good?"

The chamber was silent, very silent, as silent as the icy, frozen night outside.

"Ah dinnae knoo aboot thae," Alex said, finally. "Thae's Philosophy, an' thae's noo Scots sol'jer permitted't' think ae that, 'r thae toss him oot ae th' pub an' make him' drink piss wi' th' Brits.

"But Ah hae a wee tale. Call i' a par'ble, i' y' wish.

"Thae wae a mon. Always wanted't' prove himself, aye? An' he hears thae' th' mos' fearsome sort ae huntin' i' on Earth. Ae a wee island, i' a north' ae froze ae Vi.

"Huntin' th' bear. Cind, thae's a—"

Allan Cole

"I know what a bear is. You've called Otho one enough times. GA," she said.

"A'right. So, he goes oot i' th' forest, wi' a rifle, an' a sharp eye. An' sooner come later, he spots th' bear. Binga-banga-bonga he shoots, an' th' bear goes't doon.

"An' he bounds o'er, an' to his vast sur'prise an' dismay, thae's noo bear.

"Tap tap on th' shoulder, an' thae's th' bear! An' th' bear growls, an' says, 'If y' wan''t' live, y'll be giein' doon ae y'r nan's an' knees an' committin' a disgustin' sexual act ae m' bod'.

"An' th' hunter goes eech an' ech an' och, but th' bear's fangs ate braw, an' his claws are great. An' he goes doon ae his knees…

"Noo, when he gies back't' his camp, he's fill't wi' disgust. Wi' loathin'. He's aboot't' suicide. But first, he thinks, Ah'll hae th' skin ae thae bear!

"An' next mornin, he goes oot't' th' forest agin, an' pret' quick, he spots th' bear. An' its bompa-bompa-bompa, an' agin' th' bear goes doon.

"An' th' hunter goes clip-cloppin't' th' site, knowin' he hae th' revenge… but thae's no bear.

"Tap tap on th' shoulder… an' thae's bear! Loonrin't o'er him!

"An' th' bear says, T y' be wantin' y'r life, y'll be disrobin't, an' turnin't aroun', an' Ah'll be performin't a revoltin' sexual act wi' y'!!'

Allan Cole

"An' yeesh an' bleah an' yargh, but th' bear's claws are braw, an' his teeth are great An' so th' hunter drops hi' trews...

"Thae's it. Thae's all. Th' hunter slink't back't' camp. He feels worsen' a Campbell. H's th' lowest ae Th' low. Killin' himself i' th' best fate he c'd dream of."But firs'... th' bear mus' die! Wi' oot fail, wi'oot question.

"An' so, th' next morn, just ae dawn, th' hunter's oot i' the woods. An' agin he sees th' bear. An' again he raises his rifle. An agin i's blastawayblastawayblastaway all. An' agin' th' bear goes doon."An' agin' th' hunter rushes oop.

"An' agin', thae's noo clottin' bear!

"But agin, thae's a tap tap on th' shoulder.

"An', knowin't whae he's aboot't' see, th' hunter turns aroun'. An' thae's th' bear!

"An' th' bear eyes him up 'n down, an' says, 'Lad, y' dinnae coom f r th' huntin' noo did y'?"

Allan Cole

The Missing Jokes:

Kathryn and I looked everywhere for the following jokes. We even enlisted the help of an avid Sten reader and friend, Frank Gessel, but to no avail. Somewhere - I swear - these jokes are buried in the million plus words that make up the eight Sten novels. If anyone finds them, send an email to sten3001@aol.com and let me know so I can update this joke book in a later version. The first person to find any one of them will get a free autographed book.

Anyway, here they are:

Statues In A Park

This one is from the Real Alex Kilgour, in case you can't tell:

"Thaur ur tois statues in a park; The body ay a handsome nude cheil an' th' lovely body ay a nude girl.

"They hud bin facin' each other athwart a pathway fur a hunder years, when one bonny day an angel comes doon frae th' lift an', wi' a single gesture, brings th' tois tae life.

"The angel tells them, 'As a reward fur bein' sae patient ben a hunder blazin' summers an' dismal winters, ye hae bin given life fur thirty minutes tae dae whit yoo've wished tae dae th' most.'

"The boy statue he looks at the girl, she looks at heem, an' they gang runnin' behin' th' shrubbery.

The Missing Jokes

"Th' angel waits patiently as th' bushes rustle an' gigglin' ensues. Efter fifteen minutes , th' tois return, it ay breath an' laughin'.

"The angel tells them, 'um, ye hae fifteen minutes left. Would ye caur tae dae it again?'

"The boy statue asks the girl - 'Shaal we?'

"She eagerly replies, 'Oh, och aye, let's!

But let's change positions. Thes time, i'll hauld th' wee-pigeon doon an' ye jobby can drakh on its heed.'

*****

The Loveable Duck

A brammer wee dove is strollin' ben th' forest. And, aye, lads an' lassies, she's th' prettiest dove ye hae ever seen in yer born days. Feaithers ay pearly gray. Beak ay silver, ain dainty feit.

Ain she's happy, sae happy as she flutters alang th' path - gonnae pest a huge bramble bush.

Suddenly a big hairy arm shoots out an' grabs in th' brammer dove an' pulls 'er intae th' bushes.

The bushes shake an' shake, an' 'en shake some mair. Finally, th' arm comes out an' gently puts th' bonnie bird back oan th' forest path.

The wee spyug looks up at th' heavens, hugs herself, an' says, "I'm a dove, an' I've bin loved."

Ain aff she goes intae th' forest.

Not much later in th' day a bonnie wee bug comes skitterin' alang th' forest path. It is a brammer bug - th' loveliest in aw th'

Allan Cole

forest. Wings ay green, coopon ay gold an' a scuttle feit pretty enaw fur ballit slippers.

She hums alang th' forest path - pest 'at huir uv a sam bramble bush. Ain, lo, it comes 'at dreaded arm. Snatchin' 'er up an' pullin' 'er intae th' bushes.

The bushes shake an' shake. 'En shake some mair.

Ein 'en th' arm comes it again an' draps th' bonnie wee bug oan th' path.

She looks up at th' lift, swoonin' wi' delecht, an' she says, "I'm a bug, an' I've bin hugged."

An' aff she goes intae th' forest.

Soon enaw comes anither visitur tae uir forest. It's a bonnie duck, wi' yella' wings, an' brammer bill, an' shapely webbed feit.

As ye micht suspect, th' duck goes pest th' dreaded bramble bush. An' 'at huge hairy arm comes it, grabbin' th' duck an' pullin' it intae th' bushes.

The bushes shake an' shake. 'En shake an' shake some mair. Sae hard aw th' clottin' leaves faa tae th' grin.

Then th' arm comes out an' deposits th' duck oan th' forest path.

The bonnie bird looks up at th' lift an' says, "I'm a drake. Boy, did he make a mistake."

The End

Allan Cole

About The Sten Series

Hailed as a "landmark science fiction series" the Sten novels have thrilled millions of readers all over the world.

Set three thousand years in the future, the eight Sten novels tell the tale of a tough, street-wise orphan who escapes his fate as factory planet "delinq" to become the strong right-hand of the most powerful man in the Universe – a man hailed by his billons of subjects as "The Eternal Emperor."

THE HERO

Sten is the ultimate survivor. He's lightning quick, mean streets cunning and blessed with the twin gifts of hungry intelligence and hard-won common sense. Born on a factory planet where life has less value than the lowliest machine, Sten rebels against The Company that enslaved, then killed his parents. He finds a new family of sorts - and the means for revenge - in the ranks of the Emperor's Imperial Forces.

A series of crucial missions brings him to the attention of the Eternal Emperor himself. Sten's talents and unshakable loyalty are tested in crisis after crisis, brutal warfare, and assassination.

Besides his "black ops" skills, Sten is armed with a weapon of last resort – he carries a small knife made of an undetectable substance in a flesh and muscle "sheath" in his arm. With a blade edge only one molecule thick, the knife can cut through any substance like butter.

Sten rises swiftly until he becomes a confidante and advisor to the Emperor. Through all this Sten never forgets his lowly origins. Self-depreciating humor, friendship and luck in love

Allan Cole

shield him from Fame's blinding light. If anything his empathy and sense of responsibility for the common folk of the Empire grow with each new honor and badge of rank.

Finally he is asked to make the supreme sacrifice - risking even those he loves - to stand up for the citizens of the Empire. Then, when he succeeds, he turns his back on the greatest honor of all.

STEN'S WORLD

Picture the greatest Empire history has known. Its boundaries are the Universe itself, containing more stars, planets and sentient life than could be calculated by the swiftest 21st Century computer. This is a space kingdom where humans live side-by-side with countless alien forms. In fact the word alien itself is offensive and all species are merely called "beings." The planetary systems range from the sophistication of Prime World where the elite gather - to the rough and ready mining and frontier worlds at the Empire's edges.

Ruling over all this is:

THE ETERNAL EMPEROR

As his title implies, the Eternal Emperor is a human who has mastered death through the use of secret cloning techniques and mind transfer. When he's in his cups, he sometimes boasts that although he's been the target of hundreds of assassination, only three were successful.

The Emperor is the ultimate capitalist and when Sten steps onto the stage he has reigned for three thousand years. The source of the Eternal Emperor's power is a mysterious fuel -

82

Allan Cole

called Anti-Matter Two (AM2). It drives the star ships that link the Empire and provides the energy for all industry, agriculture and commerce. He alone controls its supply and price. And he alone knows where AM2 is to be found.

The Emperor is no tyrant. He prefers wit to force, negotiation to confrontation. But if all else fails he has enormous military resources to back up his will. His past is a rigorously guarded secret and his future is permanently entwined with the Empire he created.

Despite his vast power the Emperor greatly misses the familiar things of his 21st Century youth. On a bad day he would trade it all in for a good bottle of single malt scotch or the sweet sound of an old, hand-crafted violin. He spends his spare time in his antique-cluttered royal suites, restoring or re-constructing nostalgic objects from his salad days.

The Emperor, who has the looks of a handsome, 35-year-old, is also a consummate cook and spends hours in his Prime World kitchens recreating the recipes of ancient Earth, while hatching elaborate plans to confound his many enemies.

The Eternal Emperor sees a bit of his long ago self in Sten. After all, as he occasionally implies, his roots are as common as Sten's. If their relationship was not by necessity that of ruler and subject they might even have become friends.

Sten admires the Emperor. Perhaps, in a way, he even considers him a father figure. And he has sworn absolute loyalty to the Empire. In the end, however, he will realize that his loyalty is to the idea not the man.

Allan Cole

OTHER CHARACTERS

Sten's world is filled with bizarre and wonderful characters. Among the more important are:

ALEX KILGOUR: Sten's sidekick and confidant. An incredibly strong heavy-worlder of Scots descent, Kilgour's passion is shaggy-dog stories. All of which are so awful that his mission mates can hardly wait for the bad guys to kick in the door and interrupt him.

IAN MAHONEY: Sten's mentor. A top military man, Mahoney excels at both cloak-and-dagger and more conventional warfare, and prefers to lead from the front. He is totally loyal to Emperor.

DOC: A furry alien with the psionic talent to make people like him. It helps that humans think he's a cute, cuddly teddy-bear. Carnivorous little Doc would just love to tear their throats out for that.

IDA: The brilliant Gypsy operative (and hotrod pilot) whose hobby is making huge amounts on the stock market. She could easily retire, but she loves the challenges and danger of black operations work. Fat, mustached and foul-mouthed, she delights in harassing authority.

And there are many more, including the various beautiful and multi-talented women Sten squires during his adventures. Ranging from a tough Prime World detective, to the princess of a barbaric race of space pirates.

STREGG - THE DRINK: This heart-stopping booze appears first in Book Two: The Wolf Worlds, where the Bhor - a

84

Allan Cole

race of Viking-like beings - are introduced. Hailing from an ice-planet, their ancestral enemy was the Streggan, a fierce beast that hunted the Bohr almost into annihilation. Finally, they turned the tide and wiped out the beast entirely. They named their favorite drink Stregg, in honor of their ancient enemy. The names were inspired by a boozy session the authors' had at Harry' Bar in Century City, California. There they discovered the wonders of Stregga, the Italian liqueur. It means witch. To make Stregg for yourself, mix one part Stregg and one part white tequila. Some prefer a little simple syrup. We did not.

Allan Cole

About The Authors

International bestselling authors and screenwriters Allan Cole and the late Chris Bunch were collaborators for nearly twenty years. Together, and separately, they published over forty novels and sold more than 150 screenplays. Their most noteworthy science fiction collaboration produced the eight-book Sten series, hailed as "landmark science fiction" by Publishers Weekly, among others. For details about Allan's life and work, see his homepage at http://www.acole.com. For information about Chris, see his Wikipedia entry at http://www.en.wikipedia.org/wiki/Chris_Bunch. Both authors are also featured in the International Movie Data Base - http://www.IMDB.com . To buy the Sten series, or peruse other books by Bunch & Cole, stop by Allan's Bookstore: http://tinyurl.com/l9mpr5 And to read about their hilarious years working the gilded trenches of Tinsel Town, visit Allan's popular blog, My Hollywood MisAdventures at: http://allan-cole.blogspot.com/

###